600L

Natur

DATE DUE

V

Don

DEMCO. INC. 38-2931

Illinois

Edited by:
Jerry Stemach, MS, CCC-SLP

Gail Portnuff Venable, MS, CCC-SLP

Dorothy Tyack, MA

Consultant:
Ted S. Hasselbring, PhD

Graphics and Illustrations:
Photographs and illustrations are all created professionally
and modified to provide the best possible support for the
intended reader.
Front Cover: © Corbis
All other photos not credited here or with the photo are © Don Johnston
Incorporated and its licensors.

Narration:
Professional actors and actresses read the text to build
excitement and to model research-based elements of fluency:
intonation, stress, prosody, phrase groupings and rate.
The rate has been set to maximize comprehension for the reader.

Published by:

Don Johnston Incorporated
26799 West Commerce Drive
Volo, IL 60073

800.999.4660 USA Canada
800.889.5242 Technical Support
www.donjohnston.com

DON JOHNSTON

International Standard Book Number
ISBN-13: 978-1-58702-365-1

Contents

Chapter 1

The Sleeping Giant

Liddy Miller lived in Portland, Oregon, with her father, her mother, and her dog, Malo. Malo was a yellow lab. In 1980, Liddy was 14 years old and Malo was two years old. You could say that Liddy and Malo were the same age because one dog year is like seven human years.

Malo is the Spanish word for bad. It was the perfect word to describe Liddy's dog because Malo was always getting into trouble.

Liddy and her family loved to go camping. Liddy's father, Herb Miller, was a geologist. A geologist is a scientist who studies the earth. Mr. Miller liked to explore mountains and climb rocks. Liddy's mother, Barbara, was a photographer and she loved to fish.

On Friday, May 16, 1980, Liddy and her parents drove to the state of Washington to go camping near Mount St. Helens. Liddy's father had told her all about Mount St. Helens.

"Mount St. Helens is like a sleeping giant," Mr. Miller had said. "It has been asleep for a long time. It has not erupted for 123 years. But the giant is waking up again!" he said.

On Saturday morning, Liddy and her parents hiked to the top of a ridge above their campsite to look at Mount St. Helens. "It's over 9,500 feet tall," Mr. Miller told them. "And it's more than 40,000 years old."

The mountain was about ten miles away. It looked blue and gray, and Liddy could see some white snow at the very top. The mountain rose high above everything else around it.

"It's a beautiful mountain," Liddy thought to herself. She could also see plumes of white smoke rising from the mountain into the sky. It was exciting and a little scary to watch it.

"Is the volcano going to erupt today?" Liddy asked her father.

"It's already started to erupt,"
he replied. "The eruption began two
months ago. Now we're just waiting
for the big explosion."

Mr. Miller explained that the eruption
had started with small earthquakes
deep below the ground. Then, one side
of Mount St. Helens had started to get
bigger and bigger. "Each day the bulge
near the top of the mountain grows
a little more," he said. "There are
cracks in the bulge, and there's steam
hissing through the cracks. The snow
up there has started to melt."

There were lots of people on the ridge trail with the Millers.   Everyone was hoping that they would be lucky enough to see the big explosion. Malo seemed nervous. He barked and ran from one person to the next. When he came to Liddy, she patted him.

Mrs. Miller was looking at Mount St. Helens through her camera. "Did all the mountains around here start out as volcanoes?" she asked.

"Many of them started out as volcanoes," said Mr. Miller. "This is a land of lava."

"If Mount St. Helens exploded right this second, I would have an important photograph," said Mrs. Miller.

"You'd be famous, Mom," said Liddy. Malo barked again and ran off down the trail. "Malo!" called Liddy. "Come back here!"

"We'd better get Malo before he gets into trouble," said Mr. Miller. Liddy and her parents walked quickly down the trail and back to their campsite. "The campground is a long way from Mount St. Helens," Mr. Miller told them. "If the volcano really does explode, we'll be safe here."

Liddy could not see Mount St. Helens from their campsite, but she knew now that the sleeping giant was about ten miles to the north. She felt safe in the camp.

Liddy found Malo inside her tent. He was inside her sleeping bag. Liddy smiled. "Silly dog!" she said.

Mrs. Miller laughed, too. But Mr. Miller did not laugh. "Sometimes animals know that something is going to happen before we do," he said.

Chapter 2

A Close Call

Liddy woke up early on Sunday morning. She looked at her watch. "It's 6 o'clock on May 18," she announced to Malo. The sky slowly grew bright. Birds were singing in the forest. Liddy listened to the peaceful sounds of the nearby river. Everything else was quiet except Malo. Malo was lying on Liddy's sleeping bag and making low growling sounds.

Liddy's mother had promised to take her fishing that morning. After breakfast, Mrs. Miller showed Liddy how to tie a fishing fly onto her line.

Suddenly, the ground began to shake.
"It's an earthquake!" shouted Mr. Miller.
Liddy dropped the fly. Malo started
running. About ten seconds later,
a strong, warm wind blew past them.
Then, a huge black cloud appeared
over the ridge above them.

"Run for the truck!" Mr. Miller yelled.

Everyone jumped into the truck.
Everyone except Malo.

"Dad!" yelled Liddy. "Malo's not
here! I have to find him!" she said.

"No!" said Mr. Miller. "It's too late!"

Mr. Miller put the truck in gear and raced down the road. Liddy's eyes filled with tears. Mr. Miller was driving fast. Liddy looked behind her and saw the black cloud rolling over the campground behind them. Liddy's eyes opened wide when she saw it. "Malo is somewhere in that cloud!" she thought.

The mountain looked as if it had turned into hot liquid and smoke. The cloud rolled down the hill like a wave rolling onto the beach from the ocean.

Liddy covered her ears because the noise was louder than thunder. Trees and rocks caught fire and then disappeared into the cloud. The cloud was getting closer, and Liddy could feel the back of her head getting hotter!

"Herb!" Mrs. Miller screamed to her husband, "look out!"

The truck slammed into a large, steaming rock, and the left front tire fell off. Liddy watched the tire bounce down the road.

The brakes screeched and the truck spun around and stopped. The black cloud was coming right at them!

"Daddy!" screamed Liddy.

"Roll up the windows!" Mr. Miller yelled. Liddy rolled up the window next to her. When she looked up again, everything was dark.

The cloud had surrounded them. The truck felt like the inside of an oven that had been turned up to 500 degrees! Liddy could feel drops of sweat falling from her face.

Suddenly, there was a popping sound. One of the air vents on the truck had broken. Hot, black ash was blowing into the truck through the vent. Liddy covered her head with her hands. She felt the ash land on her bare arms. It felt like a thousand matches burning her skin. She was too scared to cry.

After a few seconds, the hot cloud passed. Then black ash started to rain down on them. The ash came down so quickly that the truck was completely covered in a few seconds. They couldn't see through the windows.

Mr. Miller put his arms around his wife and daughter. They waited for help. They were lucky that they were still alive.

"We're going to be OK," said Mr. Miller.

Liddy said only one word: "Malo."

Chapter 3

The Helicopter

Liddy sat in the truck with her mother and father for two hours before they heard the sound of a helicopter. Mr. Miller couldn't open the door, so he crawled through the window and stood on the roof. He waved his arms in the air while Liddy and her mother climbed up on the roof.

Liddy looked down at the ground. The ash was three feet deep around the truck! The explosion had been so hot that sand and other minerals had been turned into glass.

Tiny specks of glass sparkled like diamonds in the black ash.

The helicopter could not land because of all the ash on the road, so it hovered above the truck. Ash swirled in the air. A man was lowered from the helicopter on a cable. He strapped a safety harness around Liddy and they were both lifted up into the helicopter. Next came Liddy's mother and then her father.

The helicopter started to rise. The burned truck looked smaller and smaller to Liddy as they went higher.

From the air, they could really see what
had happened on the ground. All the
trees were gone. They had been swept
away by the explosion. The ground
was burned for ten miles in every
direction! Everything was covered
with black ash.

Then they saw Mount St. Helens.
The top of the mountain was gone!
The volcano had blown its top.
The bulge that had been growing
for the past two months had exploded.

Gary Braasch/CORBIS

At the top of the volcano was a huge hole called a *crater*. The crater was over a mile wide! Liddy's mother took a picture of it.

Black smoke continued to billow out of the crater. The cloud of smoke grew bigger and wider as it went up. "It looks like a giant mushroom," Liddy thought. The smoke blew toward the east. Liddy could not see how far it went.

Some of the smoke and ash and lava that came out of the crater spilled down the side of the mountain. It looked like a giant pot of soup overflowing. As the lava flowed down the mountain, it burned everything in its path. It picked up rocks and trees, and it grew bigger as it went along.

When the lava flow reached the river, some of the water from the river turned into steam. It hissed as it shot up into the sky. The river filled up with ash and trees and rocks, and the water became muddy.

The flow kept going, carrying water from the river along with it. Now the flow was more like a mudslide.

There had been a lake near Mount St. Helens called Spirit Lake. From the helicopter, Liddy could not see Spirit Lake at all. It was filled with mud, ash, rocks, and broken trees.

The helicopter flew over a forest that was owned by a logging company. All the trees here had also been blown away, and the ground was bare.

Mrs. Miller took a picture of the burned logging trucks and equipment. "Today is Sunday," she said. "It's good that the loggers are not working today. They would have been killed down there."

As the helicopter flew east, Liddy saw small craters in the ground. These craters had been made when large rocks from the explosion had hit the ground. "It looks like the surface of the moon," she told her father.

Roger Ressmeyer/CORBIS

Many bridges had also been destroyed, and some of the roads were covered by mudslides. Liddy could see people on the roads waiting for help.

At last, the helicopter landed. There were fire trucks and ambulances and police cars everywhere. As Liddy walked away from the helicopter, she saw men and women from the Army and the Red Cross. Then she saw a big black dog running toward her. It was Malo! His hair had been burned and he was covered with mud and ash.

"Is that your black lab?" a policeman asked Liddy.

Malo jumped up and licked Liddy's face. "Yes, sir!" cried Liddy. "He's supposed to be a yellow lab," she said. "But I won't complain about that."

"He came in with another family from the campground," said the policeman. "He's one lucky dog."

Chapter 4

The News on TV

A few days later, Liddy and Malo sat on the couch watching TV with Liddy's parents. The news was all about the eruption of Mount St. Helens. A reporter was talking. "The explosion has killed 57 people," he said. "And more than 125 people have been rescued."

"And one dog," said Liddy. "Don't forget our dog."

The reporter continued. "In the state of Washington, more than 100 houses were destroyed or badly damaged," he said. "At least 27 bridges and 170 miles of road have been damaged. The damage from the explosion will cost nearly 970 million dollars to repair."

The last time Mount St. Helens had erupted was 123 years ago. There was nobody still alive from that time to remind people of the danger.

This eruption was more powerful than anyone thought it would be. Even scientists like Liddy's father were surprised at the damage that it caused.

The wind had carried the smoke and ash far away. On the first day, the cloud traveled almost 4,000 miles across the United States. Before long, the cloud traveled all the way around the world!

Along the way, ash fell like snow on the ground and caused a lot of damage.

The worst damage was in the states of Washington, Idaho, and Montana. Cars and planes stopped running because the ash got into the engines. People had to wear masks to keep from getting ash into their lungs. The ash was not like snow. It did not melt. There was so much ash on the ground that many roads were closed. It would take people a long time to clean it all up.

The TV showed a picture of Mount St. Helens with smoke billowing out of the top. Mrs. Miller pointed at it and said, "That's *my* photo!"

The reporter continued. "This photo was taken by Barbara Miller of Portland, Oregon shortly after the explosion," he explained. Liddy was proud to hear her mother's name on TV.   "The photo shows what happens in a *composite* volcano," said the reporter.

"At Mount St. Helens, gasses slowly built up inside the mountain. When the pressure became too great, the volcano exploded," the reporter continued. "Gasses, dust, ash, and rocks shot from the volcano and went high into the air. The dust and ash are light so they were carried away by the wind. The rocks are heavy so they fell from the sky and slid down the sides of the mountain," he said.

Mr. Miller turned off the TV. "It's a little like shaking a can of Coke before you open it," said Mr. Miller. "The Coke explodes out of the can and goes all over the room!"

"What about the lava?" Liddy asked.

"That's a good question," replied Mr. Miller. "Lava has different names, depending on where you find it. Inside a volcano, lava is called *magma*. That's because magma comes from deep inside the earth," he said.

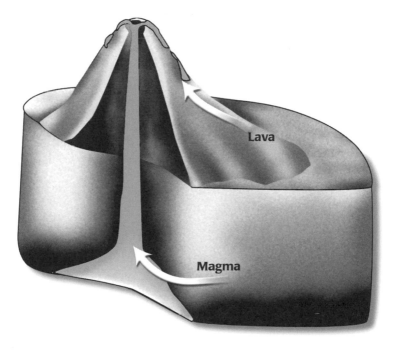

"Magma is really just a fancy word for liquid rock," explained Mr. Miller. "When magma erupts from a volcano, it's called lava. When the hot, liquid lava cools down, it's called *volcanic rock*."

"That's how mountains like Mount St. Helens are formed," Mr. Miller continued. "Magma comes out of the ground and becomes lava. The lava becomes rock and the mountain gets bigger."

Liddy rubbed her arms. They were still wrapped in bandages. They were still sore. At the hospital, the doctors had told Liddy that she would have scars on her arms from being burned by the hot ash. She hoped that the scars would not make her look ugly.

Liddy thought about all that had happened on Sunday, May 18, 1980. She scratched Malo's head. "I don't think we'll ever forget that day, Malo," she said.

Chapter 5

A Science Lesson in the Kitchen

One day after school, Liddy was in the kitchen doing homework with her mother. Mr. Miller had just come home from work. "How would you two like to go with me to see some volcanoes this summer?" he asked.

Liddy looked up from her book and answered, "Uh, Dad, I think we've already done *that*. Remember how *this* happened?" she asked. She held up her arms to show him the scars where the hot ash had burned her.

"I'm so sorry that you got hurt, Pumpkin," said Mr. Miller. "But I promise that there won't be any exploding volcanoes this time."

Malo looked up and barked. "You tell him, Malo," said Liddy. "Besides, we've already seen Mount St. Helens. Aren't all volcanoes the same?" she asked.

"Oh, no!" her father answered. "There's so much for you to learn about volcanoes that I can hardly decide where to begin."

Liddy liked to tease her father. "Make it quick, Dad, because I still have lots of homework to do," she said.

Mr. Miller opened an envelope and took out a map. He spread the map on the table. "See, here we are in Portland, Oregon," he began. "And here to the north is Mount St. Helens. But do you see this green strip that goes from Canada through Washington and Oregon and into Northern California?" he asked.

"This strip of mountains is called the Cascade Range," said Mr. Miller. "There are volcanoes all along here. And my boss wants me to study the Cascade Range this summer."

"The Cascade Range," Liddy repeated.

"Yes," said Mr. Miller. "And do you know why there are volcanoes all along the Cascade Range?"

"No, but I have a feeling that you're going to tell me," Liddy said.

"It's your lucky day!" said Mr. Miller with a smile. Mr. Miller got pretty excited when he had a chance to talk about volcanoes.

He picked up one of Liddy's notebooks and a plastic cutting board.

"What are you doing, Dad?" Liddy asked.

"Pretend that your notebook is the land at the bottom of the ocean," he said. "We call this land the *oceanic plate*."

"The cutting board is the land outside the ocean," he explained. "This land is part of a continent, so we call it a *continental plate*. The two plates are pushing against each other, and the oceanic plate is being forced under the continental plate. Like this," said Mr. Miller.

He placed the cutting board over the sink. Then he put the notebook just below the edge of the cutting board. Then he started pushing the notebook into the sink.

"I don't think you need to do this experiment over the sink, Dad," said Liddy.

"Yes, I do," said Mr. Miller. "I want you to pretend that the sink is the inside of the earth," he continued. "Now, the inside of the earth is very hot and filled with..." Mr. Miller stopped. "Liddy, do you remember what lava is called when it is still inside the earth?" he asked.

"Magma," Liddy answered.

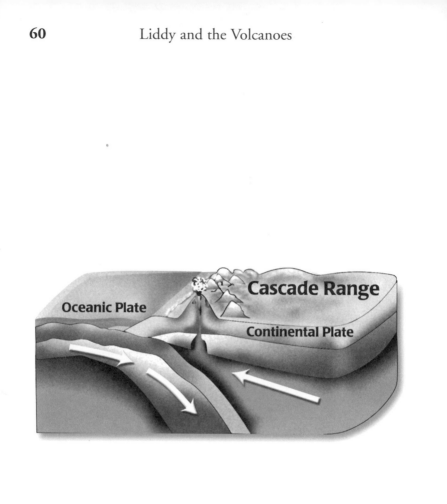

"That's right! The inside of the earth is filled with magma. What's another name for magma, Liddy?" he asked.

"Liquid rock," replied Liddy.

"Exactly," said Mr. Miller. He pushed the notebook farther into the sink with the cutting board. "Do you see what's happening? The oceanic plate is pushed below the continental plate. In real life, it happens very slowly. It's been going on for millions of years," he said.

"When the oceanic plate goes down deep into the magma, it gets so hot that it melts," he continued. "All of that hot magma needs a place to go, and hot things want to go up. So the magma breaks through the weak spots in the continental plate and shoots out of the earth. And presto! That's how the volcanoes of the Cascade Range were born," he said.

"Wow, that's really cool, Dad," said Liddy.

"No, it's really hot," kidded Mr. Miller.

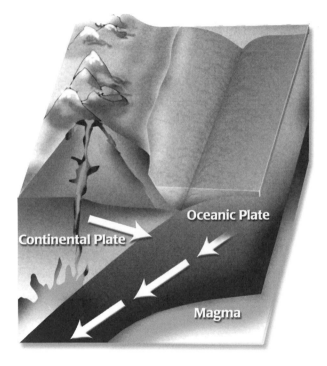

"So, what do you say? Do you want to go and see some volcanoes with me this summer?"

"Can we go, Mom?" Liddy asked.

"Only if there are some good places to go trout fishing," Mrs. Miller answered. "Now let's finish your homework," she said. "I don't want any more eruptions or interruptions from either my husband or your dog."

Chapter 6

A Mountain and a Crater

National Archives

That summer, Liddy's family and Malo took a trip through part of the Cascade Mountain Range. From Portland, they drove southeast to Mount Hood. Liddy had seen Mount Hood from her home because Mount Hood is only 45 miles from Portland. But this was the first time that she had ever visited the mountain.

Mrs. Miller was looking at a book about volcanoes. "Mount Hood is 11,000 feet tall. It's the tallest mountain in Oregon," she read aloud.

It was cold and windy high up on Mount Hood. The ground was made of dark, gray volcanic rock, and it was covered with snow and ice. Malo ran through the snow. He kept sliding on the patches of ice and falling over.

Liddy could see the Cascade Range spread out in front of her. The ridges and valleys looked as if they went on forever. The clouds seemed so close that Liddy wanted to reach up and touch them.

"The Cascade Range begins way up in British Columbia, Canada," explained her father. "Meager Mountain is the farthest north, then comes Mount Garibaldi in southern British Columbia."

He handed Liddy a pair of binoculars. To the north, she could see Mount St. Helens in the state of Washington.

"There are other big volcanoes in Washington besides Mount St. Helens," her father continued.

CORBIS

"There's Mount Baker, Glacier Peak, Mount Adams, and Mount Rainier," he explained. "Then, behind you, there are more big volcanoes here in Oregon. We'll be visiting a volcano called Crater Lake in Oregon. If we get as far south as California, we'll see Mount Shasta and Lassen Peak."

"I didn't know that there were so many volcanoes on the west coast of the United States," said Liddy.

"There are hundreds of them if you count the small ones," he said. "Most of them are dormant. That means they haven't erupted for a few thousand years."

"I know one thing," said Liddy. "Mount St. Helens isn't dormant!"

"Mount St. Helens and Mount Lassen are the only volcanoes in the Cascade Range that have erupted in the past 100 years," said Mr. Miller.

"They're called active volcanoes,"
he said. "Scientists also call Mount
Baker and Mount Rainier active
because they may erupt within the
next few hundred years."

Next, the Millers drove down
to Crater Lake. When Liddy got out
of the car, she could see that the lake
was at the bottom of a steep hill.
Malo ran toward the water.

"Cool lake, but where's the
volcano?" Liddy asked her father.

CORBIS

"You're looking at it," he replied. "Crater Lake used to be a volcano called Mount Mazama. About 7,000 years ago, Mount Mazama exploded. The explosion was even more powerful than Mount St. Helens. Mount Mazama shot out so much magma that the top of the volcano fell in because there was nothing left to hold it up! Craters made by volcanoes that collapse like that are called *calderas*," he explained. "Caldera is a Spanish word that means 'kettle.' The crater on Mount St. Helens is over one mile wide, but this crater is almost six miles wide."

Liddy looked at the lake through the binoculars. Then she spoke in Spanish. *"Malo está en la caldera,"* she said.

"I don't speak Spanish," said Mrs. Miller. "But let me see if I understand. 'Malo is in the lake.' "

"Yep," said Liddy, "something like that."

"It's a steep trail down to the lake," said Mr. Miller. "I don't mind going down. It's the hike back up that worries me."

Mrs. Miller put some sandwiches into her backpack. "Let's go and get Malo," she said. "He'll stay in Crater Lake for a week if we don't go down there."

During the hike to the lake, Mr. Miller told a story about the Klamath Indians. "The Klamath Indians were the first people to live here," he said. "They believed that a good god named Skell fought against an evil god in this place. The two gods threw fireballs at each other and Skell killed the evil god," explained Mr. Miller.

"Then Skell dug up the top of this mountain and buried his enemy," continued Mr. Miller. "The Klamath Indians believed that the rain came and filled up the hole to make this lake."

Malo loved to swim, but he loved to eat even more. Liddy called to him and held up part of her cheese sandwich, and he ran right over to her. He was dripping wet. Malo stood next to Mr. and Mrs. Miller, shook cold water all over them, and then ran off with the bag of potato chips.

Chapter 7

Mount Vesuvius

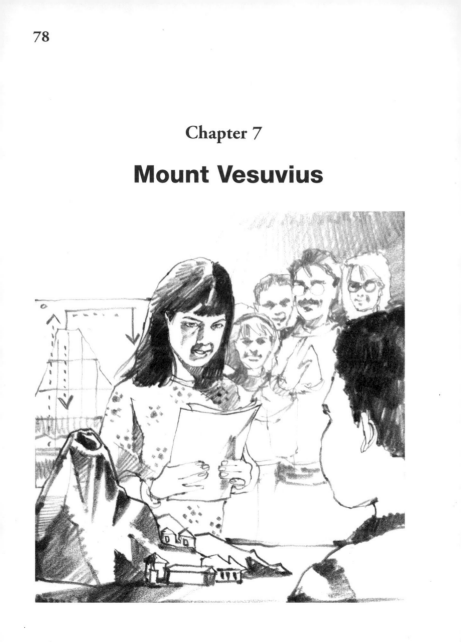

When Liddy was in the tenth grade, she decided to be in the school science fair. Her trip to the Cascade Range made her want to learn more about volcanoes, and the science fair gave her a chance to do it.

Liddy's father told her about a famous volcano in Italy named Mount Vesuvius. "Mount Vesuvius completely buried two cities," he told her.

"You could make a model of Vesuvius," her father said. "I can get some chemicals to make a real eruption!"

"Now that would be cool!" said
Liddy.

"No," her father laughed, "that
would be hot."

Liddy's parents helped her to make
a model of Mount Vesuvius. First,
they put an empty glass bottle on top
of a large board. Next, they put wire
and plaster around the bottle. Liddy
shaped the plaster to look like
a volcano. Then, she painted the model
with brown, black, and gray paint.

At the bottom of the model, Liddy made two towns out of cardboard. Then, Mr. Miller put some chemicals inside the glass bottle.

The day of the science fair, Liddy stood next to her model of Mount Vesuvius. Liddy had written a short report for her project. When the judges came to see her project, Liddy read her report to them.

"My name is Liddy Miller and my science project is on volcanoes," she said. "I was in the Mount St. Helens explosion, and the hot ash burned my arms." Liddy held up her arms for everyone to see. Then she continued.

"The word 'volcano' comes from the name of a small island in Italy. A long time ago, people believed that a god named Vulcan lived on the island. Vulcan was a blacksmith, and he used fire to make weapons. People believed that the volcano was Vulcan's chimney."

"Mount Vesuvius is a famous volcano in Italy. It is a composite volcano, so it looks a lot like Mount St. Helens," Liddy explained. "Mount St. Helens surprised a lot of people when it erupted, and so did Mount Vesuvius. Mount Vesuvius's most famous eruption happened in the year 79. That was almost 2,000 years ago."

"Back then, people thought that Mount Vesuvius must be dormant because it had not erupted for hundreds of years," said Liddy.

"There were plants and animals living on the mountain. And there were two cities named Pompeii and Herculaneum nearby," Liddy continued.

"In the year 63, there were earthquakes below the volcano, but people did not pay attention to them. Then, in the year 79, Mount Vesuvius exploded. There was so much ash from Mount Vesuvius that the cities of Pompeii and Herculaneum were buried for 1,700 years. They were not found until the year 1748!"

By the time Liddy finished reading her report out loud, there was a large crowd around her table.

"Now, who wants to see Mount Vesuvius erupt?" Liddy asked the crowd.

The people came closer to Liddy's volcano. Liddy pointed to a picture that she had made. The picture showed the inside of a volcano.

"The inside of a real volcano is similar to my model volcano," Liddy told the crowd.

"In the center of a real volcano, there is a hollow tube," she explained. It is called the 'central vent.' When lava flows out of the top, it slides down the sides of the mountain and becomes rock as it cools. Now, watch this!" she said.

Liddy put on safety glasses and lit a match. She put the match in the opening of her model volcano. Black smoke began to come out of the top. There was a lot of sulfur in the smoke. The sulfur smelled like smoke from burning matches.

"This is what an erupting volcano really smells like!" Liddy told the crowd.

Sparks came out of the top of Liddy's volcano. The crowd took a step back. Then, a flame shot out of the model volcano, and lava came running down the sides of Liddy's mountain. The lava covered the two cardboard towns at the bottom.

The crowd clapped their hands when Liddy's volcano stopped erupting. The judges put a blue ribbon on Liddy's volcano. She had won first prize at the science fair!

Chapter 8

The Big Picture

After Liddy graduated from high school, she went away to college. She was 18 years old. Liddy was going to study volcanoes at the University of Hawaii. She wanted to be a geologist like her father.

"I'm proud of you, Pumpkin," Mr. Miller told her at the airport.

Liddy's mother gave her a hug and said, "Take care of yourself, Liddy."

"Thanks for everything, Mom and Dad," Liddy said. "Don't worry about me. I'll send you an e-mail every week!"

Liddy gave Malo one last pat. "Good-bye, Malo," said Liddy. "I wish that I could take you with me. But there's so much water around Hawaii that you'd be in trouble *all* the time," she said. Malo barked.

Liddy closed her eyes as the plane took off. This would be her first time away from her parents.

Liddy's favorite teacher in college was a German man named Dr. Robert Keller. Everyone called him Dr. Einstein because he looked like the famous scientist, Dr. Albert Einstein. Dr. Keller was a short man with wild, frizzy hair, and he spoke with a German accent. Dr. Keller was a scientist like Liddy's father.

The first thing Dr. Keller told his class was this: "Volcanoes destroy and volcanoes create. Remember that." The students wrote his words down in their notebooks.

"Now, what does that mean?" he asked.

Liddy raised her hand.

Dr. Keller looked at her and said, "Tell us your name and where you come from. That way, we will become friends here."

Liddy spoke. "I'm Liddy Miller, from Portland, Oregon. I think you mean that volcanoes can cause a lot of damage," she replied.

"But volcanoes also help to create much of the earth's surface. I read that 80% of the earth's surface was made by volcanoes," said Liddy.

Dr. Keller moved his bushy eyebrows in surprise. "Good answer, Liddy," he said. Then he pointed to a map on the wall. "What Liddy said is true. 80% for the world, but 100% for Hawaii. These small dots on the map are the Hawaiian Islands. They are in the middle of the Pacific Ocean, and every island here was made by volcanoes."

A boy in the back row spoke. "I'm James Kapono from the Big Island," he said.

Liddy knew that "the Big Island" was another name for the island of Hawaii, which is the biggest of all the Hawaiian Islands. The University of Hawaii was on the Big Island. Liddy knew that there were many active volcanoes on this island.

"How could there be so many volcanoes in just one spot in the Pacific Ocean?" asked James.

"Good question, James," said Dr. Keller. "The answer is *plate tectonics*. Let me explain."

Dr. Keller explained that the earth's surface is broken into about 12 plates of land. Each plate is about 50 miles thick. "The plates are moving apart in some places, and they are crashing into each other in other places. Most volcanoes are near where these plates meet or move apart," he said.

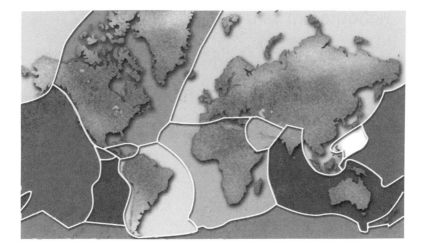

"There are volcanoes all around the Pacific Ocean," Dr. Keller continued. "That's why we call it the 'Ring of Fire.' There are volcanoes on the west coast of North America and South America, in Alaska, along the coasts of Russia and East Asia, and next to Australia. These are places where the oceanic plate is being forced underneath the continental plates."

Liddy remembered her father's example with the cutting board and the notebook in the kitchen sink.

She thought about how the Cascade Range had been formed. Now she could see that the Cascade Range was part of the Ring of Fire.

"Is that how the Hawaiian islands were made?" Liddy asked.

"No, Hawaii is different," Dr. Keller said. "The Hawaiian islands were made by a *hot spot*. A hot spot is a hole in the oceanic plate where magma comes out from inside the earth. If you hold a thin piece of wood over a flame, the fire burns a hole in the wood, right?" he asked.

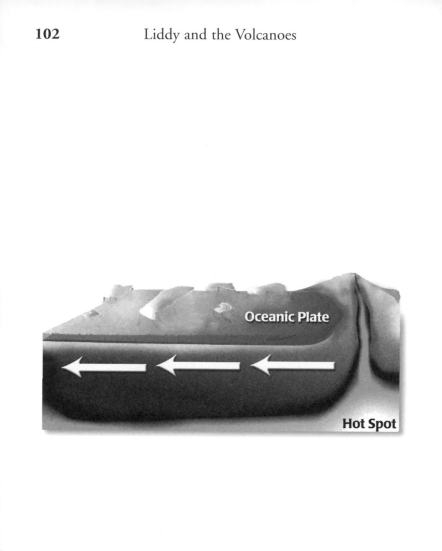

"If you keep moving the wood over the fire, it makes more holes," said Dr. Keller. "The oceanic plate has been moving over this hot spot for millions of years. Each island was formed by lava coming up through a hole in the oceanic plate. That is why the Hawaiian islands are made of 100% volcanic rock."

"OK, I understand," Liddy said. She was putting everything together in her mind. She was starting to get the big picture.

Chapter 9

Lava Lake

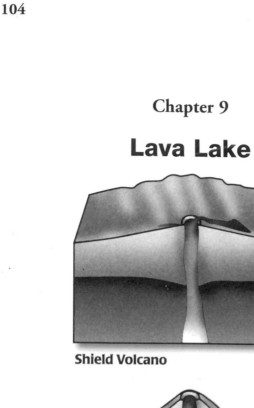

Shield Volcano

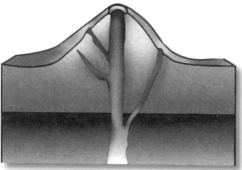

Composite Volcano

Dr. Keller took his class on a field trip to Hawaii Volcanoes National Park. The park is located between two big volcanoes — Mauna Loa and Kilauea. They are two of the most active volcanoes in the world. In fact, Kilauea was erupting when they arrived at the park.

Dr. Keller explained that these volcanoes are called *shield* volcanoes. "They are different from composite volcanoes like Mount St. Helens," he explained.

"Composite volcanoes are shaped like a cone with a pointy top. But shield volcanoes are round like a hill," Dr. Keller continued. "Composite volcanoes and shield volcanoes have different shapes because they have different types of eruptions."

"In the Mount St. Helens eruption, there were rocks and lava and a thick cloud of smoke and black ash," said Liddy.

"Yes," replied Dr. Keller. "That's what happens with a composite volcano. But when a shield volcano like Kilauea erupts, it is almost all lava. The lava runs down the side of the volcano like water that is spilling out of a bathtub."

"The lava here is like thick red syrup. It's moving very slowly," said Dr. Keller. "But it can move a long way. Some of this lava is spilling into the ocean," he said.

"A shield eruption can last for a long time. That is why a shield volcano can get so big. They can be many miles wide. But you won't see much smoke or ash when they erupt," he said.

Dr. Keller wanted to climb up the volcano and get a sample of the hot lava. "We'll be right next to the molten lava," he said. "Stay with a partner and be careful. I don't want to barbecue any students today," he kidded them. Liddy laughed, but she remembered what had happened to her arms, and walked slowly.

Liddy walked with James, the
student from the Big Island. As they
climbed up Kilauea, Liddy noticed two
types of volcanic rock. One type
of rock was smooth. It looked like
lumpy thick paint that had dried. And
sometimes the rock looked like rows
of thick rope. The other kind of rock
was rough and sharp. "My tennis
shoes wouldn't last long on that!"
she told James.

As they got near the top of Kilauea, they saw a plume of smoke. Then they saw a large crater in the middle of a field. In the middle of the crater was a cinder cone. Around the edge of the cone was a crust of black lava that was cooling. Bright red lava was spilling though the cracks in the black crust. Soon, the crater was filled with bubbling red lava.

"This is the lava lake," Dr. Keller announced.

Dr. Keller, Liddy, and James walked to the edge of the lava lake. It was so hot that Liddy had to cover her face with her hand. She could smell her tennis shoes starting to melt. Molten lava was still spilling out of the crater.

"We must hurry," Dr. Keller said.

He took a small shovel and dug it into the lake. Then they walked back to where the rest of the students were waiting. The red lava in the shovel was starting to cool and turn black. Dr. Keller dropped it into a metal bucket with a clang.

"OK," Dr. Keller said. "Let's go before we all melt like snowmen."

The sun was starting to set and the clouds in the sky were turning yellow and red and purple. The class had planned to cook hamburgers for dinner and have a party. Dr. Keller and the rest of the students took food and surfboards from the van and went to the beach. Liddy and James stayed by the van for a while.

The clouds began to drift away.
Liddy and James could see a gigantic
gray mountain appear from behind
the clouds.

"That's Mauna Loa," James said.

"Wow, it makes me feel so small!"
said Liddy. "It must be four times
as tall as Kilauea!"

"And we can't even see half of it,"
James said. "There's even more
of the mountain under the ocean."

Liddy liked James. He was the first boy she had met who enjoyed volcanoes as much as she did. "I read that Mauna Loa is the largest mountain in the world," Liddy said.

"That's right," James answered. "It's more than 13,000 feet tall. And there is another 18,000 feet under the water."

It was almost dark now. Liddy could see the river of molten lava spilling into the ocean. She looked up at Mauna Loa.

Now she understood why people
of long ago had believed that gods
lived on mountaintops and inside
the earth. Liddy grabbed James
by the hand and they ran to the beach.

Chapter 10

Mount Pinatubo Erupts!

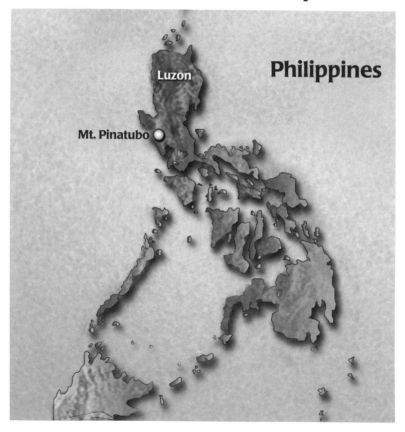

In the summer of 1991, Liddy and James were helping Dr. Keller with his work. Dr. Keller was going to the Philippines to study volcanoes. He wanted Liddy and James to go with him. "I could use your help," he told them.

The Philippines are a group of islands in Southeast Asia. Liddy, James, and Dr. Keller met some other scientists on the island of Luzon. "We have come to Luzon because Mount Pinatubo is erupting," Dr. Keller told them.

"Mount Pinatubo is a composite volcano like Mount St. Helens," explained Dr. Keller. "About 11 years ago, the eruption at Mount St. Helens began with small earthquakes. Now there are earthquakes underneath Mount Pinatubo. The earthquakes are getting stronger every day," he said.

By the time Dr. Keller, Liddy, and James arrived, there were hundreds of small earthquakes every day below the volcano. They could see steam rising from Mount Pinatubo. The big explosion would come soon.

There were people living all around Mount Pinatubo. The mountain had not erupted for 400 years. It had not erupted for so long that the people living nearby thought it was just another mountain. They did not believe that they were in danger. The scientists had to warn the people and get them out of their homes before the volcano exploded.

On June 12, the government leaders told all the people living near Mount Pinatubo to move to a safer place.

A total of 58,000 people had to move. It took three days to get all the people out of the villages on buses.

Mount Pinatubo exploded on June 15, just as the last people were leaving.

Liddy and Dr. Keller were at a nearby U.S. Air Force base. They saw the cloud of ash and smoke grow like a giant mushroom above the volcano. James was on his way to join them at the base. Liddy and Dr. Keller watched the lava flow run down the side of the mountain.

The lava destroyed everything in its path. When it reached a river, it became a mudslide. All of the villages below would be swept away.

Suddenly, Liddy heard a voice on the walkie-talkie.

"Help! Can anyone hear me? I'm on the road to the base, but my truck won't start!" the voice said.

"It's James!" cried Liddy.

The volcanic mudslide was heading straight for him!

"We have to save him!" Dr. Keller exclaimed.

James was standing on the roof of his truck when the helicopter came. Liddy was lowered from the helicopter on a cable. She could see that the mudslide was moving quickly down the road.

"Hurry!" yelled James.

Liddy was at the end of the cable, but the cable was just a little too short. She couldn't reach James. The helicopter couldn't go any lower because there were tall trees in the way.

"Jump up and grab my arm!" Liddy yelled.

James jumped, and Liddy caught him by his wrist. At that moment, the mudslide hit the truck and swept it away. James was too low!

His feet were caught in the mudslide, and it started to pull him away, but Liddy held onto him tightly. She looked up at the helicopter. The pilot started to go up. Dr. Keller pulled in the cable and brought Liddy and James up to safety.

"That was a close call!" Dr. Keller said to them. He hugged them and Liddy could see tears in his eyes.

"We're all OK," she said.

Liddy invited James to come to Oregon with her. The next day, she and James were on an airplane back to Hawaii. From there, they took a plane to Portland. After a long day of flying, they saw that they were over the Cascade Range.

"Now, Mr. James Kapono," said Liddy. "Look down there. Let me show you the volcanoes where I live."

The End

About the Author

Godwin Chu is a San Francisco writer who now lives in New York City. He was born in Rangoon, Burma, in 1972. When he was five years old, Godwin and his family came to the United States. When he is not writing stories for Start-to-Finish, he works as an editor at Columbia University Press in New York City.

Godwin also enjoys hiking, riding his bicycle, listening to music, and watching baseball games.